Oliver Elephant

For my lovely parents
L. P.

To Santa's elves, who help make
Christmas a magical time
H. S.

First U.S. edition 2018

Library of Congress Catalog Card Number pending
ISBN 978-1-5362-0266-3

18 19 20 21 22 23 WKT 10 9 8 7 6 5 4 3 2 1

Printed in Shenzhen, Guangdong, China

This book was typeset in Adobe Caslon Pro.
The illustrations were done in various media.

Nosy Crow
an imprint of
Candlewick Press
99 Dover Street
Somerville, Massachusetts 02144

www.nosycrow.com
www.candlewick.com

Oliver Elephant

Lou Peacock

illustrated by Helen Stephens

An imprint of Candlewick Press

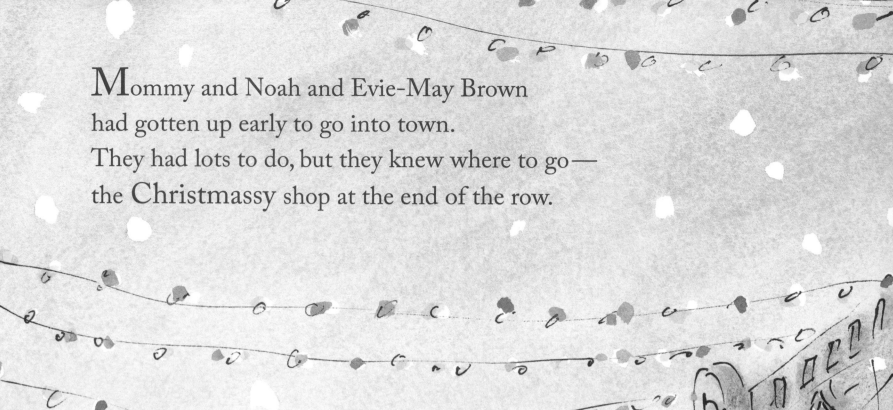

Mommy and Noah and Evie-May Brown
had gotten up early to go into town.
They had lots to do, but they knew where to go—
the Christmassy shop at the end of the row.

"Look, Mommy!" said Noah. "This shop is so **tall**! I bet it makes Evie-May feel very small. But Oliver Elephant's terribly brave."

"Of course," Mommy said, "and I'm **sure** he'll behave."

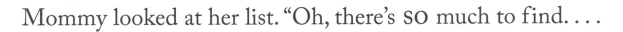

Mommy looked at her list. "Oh, there's so much to find. . . .

We need something for Mary—
she's always so kind.

A gift for Aunt Mabel,
and something that's maybe
quite little for Emma—
she's only a baby.

We need something for Chloe
and something for Claire,
and for Great Uncle Jock—
perhaps something to wear.

And Grandma has asked
us to please have a look
for something for Granddad,
who's learning to cook.

"There's something else, too—
but, oh, what can it be?"
"I know!" Noah said.
"It's the **star** for the tree!"

And so they set off,
Mommy leading the way,
past tall rows of shelves
and a pretty display.

While Mommy bought warm gloves
for Great Uncle Jock . . .

Oliver Elephant tried on a sock.

While Mommy found Emma
a tiny toy mouse . . .

Oliver Elephant hid in a house.

While Mommy found Granddad
Good Cooking For Two . . .

Oliver Elephant played
peekaboo.

While Mommy bought lavender soap for Aunt Mabel . . .

Oliver Elephant danced on the table.

While Mommy found
Mary an elegant mug . . .

Oliver Elephant bumped
a glass jug.

And while Mommy bought chocolates for Chloe and Claire . . .

Oliver Elephant slumped on a chair.

"Thank goodness,"
said Mommy,
"we're finally done!
Let's all go downstairs
for a cinnamon bun."

"Are you hungry?" said Mommy.
"Don't these buns look nice?"
But Noah picked out
a big chocolaty slice!

Then Mommy and Noah
and Evie-May Brown
found somewhere to sit,
and they put their things down.

Noah finished his cake.
Mommy put down her cup.
Evie-May was tucked in.
All the bags were picked up.

They put on their coats and were ready to leave . . .

when **suddenly**
Noah tugged hard
at Mom's sleeve.

"Where's Oliver Elephant,
Mommy? Oh, no!
We've lost him!
HE'S GONE!

Mommy, where did he go?"

"Oh, Noah," said Mommy, "please, darling, don't cry.

We'll find him in no time. Come on now, let's try."

And so they set off, Noah leading the way,
to check all the places they'd been to that day.

They **rushed** to the chocolate shop
first—just in case.

And **looked** inside vases.
(There **might** have been space.)

They **checked** under tables
piled high with shampoo.

And **peered** behind bookshelves
and customers, too.

They **searched** between teddy bears
lined up in rows.

They **ran** back to menswear
and looked through the clothes.

They searched the whole store.
They had looked **everywhere**.

But Oliver Elephant
just wasn't there.

"Oliver Elephant, where can you be?
Oliver Elephant, come back to me!"

Then, "Wait!" Mommy called out.
"What's wrong, Evie-May?
Quick, Noah, come here!
She has something to say."

Then Evie-May wriggled, and **what** should appear . . .

but a crumpled blue **trunk** and a velvety **ear**.

"My elephant!"
Noah yelled,
spinning around.

"I thought you were lost!
I'm so happy you're found!"

As Mommy and Noah and Evie-May Brown
were ready to leave, Mommy stopped with a frown.

"There's something we've missed—but, oh,
what can it be?"

"I know!" Noah said . . .

"It's the **star** for the tree."

Linda Meeker of @greyandmama stumbled upon social media popularity as she shared sweet videos of her son Grey learning to say "thank you." Expressing gratitude was a value instilled in Linda as a child raised in a Vietnamese family, so she was delighted that the simple act of her toddler saying "thank you" received such a reaction on TikTok and Instagram. Linda, her husband, and Grey live in Seattle, Washington.

"We had a lot of different foods today," Mama said. "Did you decide your favorite?"

"That's easy," Grey said. "Right now my favorite food is pineapple. Because my favorite food is anything I'm sharing with you or Dada or Ngoại or Auntie or Rambo."

"Thank you, Grey!

That is Mama's favorite food too."

"I love dinner!" Grey cheered.

"This is so yummy.

Thank you, Mama!

Thank you, Dada!

Cảm ơn, Ngoại!

Thank you, Auntie!"

He brought a big bottle of spice for Mama. Kimchi for Dada. Lettuce and herbs for Ngoại. And salty seaweed for Auntie.

These must be their favorite foods, Grey thought.

Mama chopped green onions. Dada measured the rice.
Ngoại cooked the fish in a caramel glaze. Auntie cooked
the veggies. And Grey set the table.

He just couldn't decide what his favorite food was.

"I'm still not sure, Mama," Grey said. "But can we have rice and fish for dinner? And some seaweed?"

"Of course we can. That's Ngoọi's favorite dinner!" Mama said.

"What's your favorite food for dinner?" Mama asked.

Hmmm, Grey wondered. He loved brothy ramen. And he really liked salads with bright-red tomatoes and sweet peppers that snapped in his teeth. And saucy noodles with tofu. Then there were spring rolls with delicious sweet-and-salty peanut sauce.

Then Grey heard the rumble again. But it wasn't Rambo this time.

"Mama, I think it's time for dinner!" Grey said.

"I think you're right," Mama said. "And for Dada and Ngọại and Auntie too."

Later, as he and Rambo landed their ship, Captain Grey heard a strange sound. Was it a sea monster? No. It was Rambo's belly!

And  with Ngoại?

And  with Auntie?

And **apples**
with Rambo?

Hmmm, Grey thought as he chewed the tangy tuna salad and soft, sweet bread. Was a tuna sandwich his favorite food?

But what about
bubble tea
with Mama?

And **donuts**
with Dada?

"A tuna sandwich!" Grey said. "Is a tuna sandwich my favorite food, Mama?"

"What do *you* think?" Mama asked.

"Remember, you have to decide for yourself."

"Let's make a sandwich," Mama said. "What kind would you like?"

Hmmm, Grey thought. He loved peanut butter and jelly sandwiches. And ham and cheese. And he especially liked tuna sandwiches.

Grey thought of all the foods he liked for lunch.

"Mama, what's for lunch?" Grey asked.

After a while, the rumbling, tumbling, grumbling sound returned.

RRRR-RERR-RR

And flaky **crackers**
with **cheese**.

And sweet
mangoes.

Hmmm, Grey thought as he chomped on a crunchy pickle.
These foods were delicious.

But he also liked
salted edamame.

And leafy broccoli.

And crispy
seaweed.

Mama gave Grey a plate filled with tart olives, sour pickles, buttery chestnuts, silky smooth cheese, and crisp apples.

"Thank you, Mama.

We're going to eat it all up!"

"Is this your favorite snack, Grey?" Mama asked.

After Firefighter Grey saved the day,
he asked Mama, "May I have olives and
pickles and chestnuts and cheese?
And some apples for Rambo?"

"Of course. That's a
good snack,
Grey!" Mama said.

Grey wondered what his favorite snack might be.

After breakfast, Grey and Rambo played pretend. But being a hero is hard work. Grey's stomach rumbled, tumbled, and grumbled.

"Let's make pancakes today, and then you can decide," Mama said. "What should we put on top?"

"Whipped cream and sprinkles," Grey said. "And lots of sweet, juicy berries."

"Hooray for pancakes! Thank you, Mama!"

"Are pancakes your favorite breakfast food?" Mama asked.

"I like pancakes!"
Grey said.

"But I don't know if
they are my favorite."

But he also really liked cereal.

And oatmeal.

And eggs.

And yogurt with bananas and strawberries.

"I don't know," Grey said. "What is my favorite food, Mama?"

"I can't tell you that, silly," Mama said. "A favorite is something you decide for yourself."

"What's your favorite food for breakfast?" Mama asked.

Hmmm, Grey thought.

He loved toast with creamy bright-green avocado on top.

And he loved pancakes with whipped cream and fruit.

Breakfast!

"Mama, can we have something special for breakfast?" Grey asked.

"Oh, yes," Mama said. "Breakfast is my favorite meal."

"It's my favorite too!" Grey cheered. "What will we have?"

SLURP, SLOOP, SLUUUP!

Rambo!

It must be morning, Grey thought.
And morning means . . .

Grey woke up to a familiar, funny feeling on his toes.

For Mom—Cảm ơn for every lesson of gratitude, both big and small.

For Matt—In every lifetime, I will find my way back to you.

For Grey—My literal beating heart—I don't know how I ever lived without you.

For Rambo—Thank you for thirteen beautiful years. We'll miss you forever.

—L.M.

For my mama, Su-Ying, and my dog, Moon.

—S.E.

Grey thanks his grandmother by saying,
"Cảm ơn, Ngoại!" *Cảm ơn* is Vietnamese
for *thank you*. Say it like this: cahm-un.
Ngoại is Vietnamese for *grandmother*.
Say it like this: n-gwai.

Library of Congress Cataloging-in-Publication Data

Names: Meeker, Linda, 1984- author. | Eide, Sandra, illustrator.
Title: Thank you, Mama / Linda Meeker ; illustrated by Sandra Eide.
Description: Nashville, TN : Thomas Nelson, [2022] | Audience: Ages 3-7 | Summary: "As Grey enjoys meals and snacks, he wonders which is his favorite food. Trying veggies and fruit, quinoa and sushi, Grey discovers the power of food to connect us to those we love"-- Provided by publisher.
Identifiers: LCCN 2021046173 (print) | LCCN 2021046174 (ebook) | ISBN 9781400231454 (hardcover) | ISBN 9781400231492 (epub)
Subjects: CYAC: Food--Fiction. | Gratitude--Fiction. | LCGFT: Picture books.
Classification: LCC PZ7.1.M4667 Th 2022 (print) | LCC PZ7.1.M4667 (ebook) | DDC [E]--dc23
LC record available at https://lccn.loc.gov/2021046173
LC ebook record available at https://lccn.loc.gov/2021046174

Illustrated by Sandra Eide

Printed in South Korea

22 23 24 25 26 SAM 6 5 4 3 2 1

Mfr: SAM / Seoul, South Korea / March 2022 / PO# 12060306

Thank You,
Mama

WRITTEN BY
Linda Meeker
OF @GREYANDMAMA

ILLUSTRATED BY
Sandra Eide

An Imprint of Thomas Nelson